THE HORSE WHO HAD HIS PICTURE IN THE PAPER

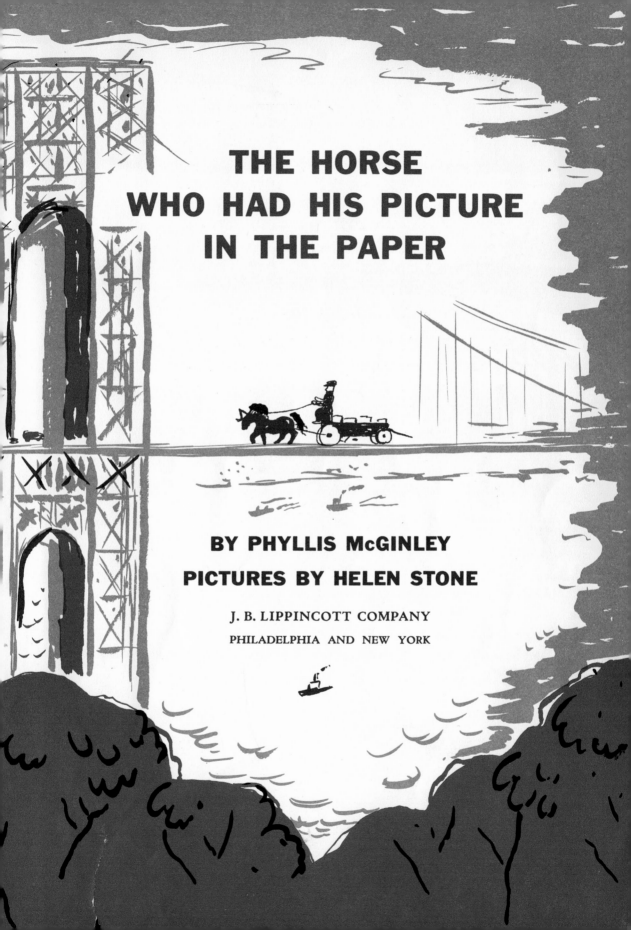

THE HORSE
WHO HAD HIS PICTURE
IN THE PAPER

BY PHYLLIS McGINLEY
PICTURES BY HELEN STONE

J. B. LIPPINCOTT COMPANY

PHILADELPHIA AND NEW YORK

Library of Congress Catalog Card Number 51-11174

There is a city called New York, so crowded with tall buildings that you must tilt back
your head and look straight up to see the sky.

So of course there isn't room for green
fields or fat red barns. Nearly everybody lives
upstairs—even the horses.

In one of the buildings lived a horse named Joey.

Joey was a contented horse. He liked his upstairs stable and he liked his stall, which was sunny, with a window to look out of.

He liked working for Mr. Polaski who sold fruit and vegetables to city people.

He liked the folks he met as he pulled his cart about the city streets.

And he was fond of his friend, the Percheron, who lived in the left-hand stall.

In fact, he was as contented as a horse can be, until the day that Brownie moved into the right-hand stall next door to his.

Brownie was a Police Horse, and he never let anyone forget it. He was shining brown all over except for his mane and his tail, which were black. And he was very proud. He was proud of his mane and proud of his tail and proud of being on the Force. And he was very, *very* proud because he had had his picture in the paper.

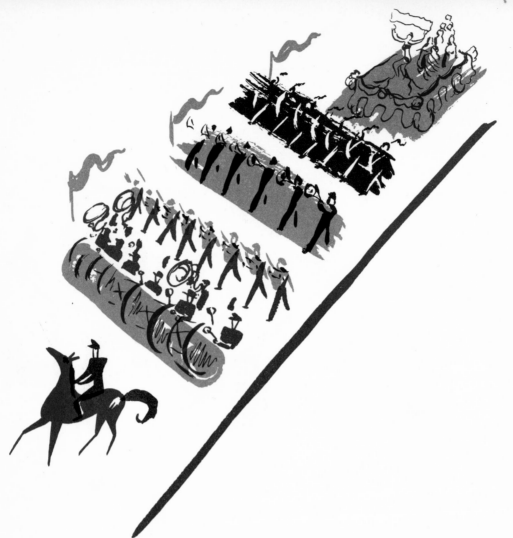

He treated the other horses coolly because they were ordinary fellows who pulled carts like Joey or hauled great drays like the Percheron. He himself carried a Police Sergeant on his back and was much admired by all the passersby.

Sometimes he led parades up Fifth Avenue and sometimes he kept the crowds in order when something exciting was going on. And he had

been to school to learn how to jump over bars and how not to be afraid of loud noises, and how to act like a policeman.

"It isn't just any horse who gets on the Force," he told Joey haughtily. "We're picked for our brains, you know. Besides, I'm a hero. That's why I had my picture in the paper."

"Is that good?" asked Joey, who had lived a sheltered life.

"Of course it's good," said Brownie. "It got my Sergeant a promotion. So now he has more money in the bank and I have more apples with my lunch."

Joey didn't care about the apples. Mr. Polaski gave him all the apples he wanted, anyhow. But he knew that Mr. Polaski had six children at home who were always needing new shoes, and that sometimes he was worried about money. "A vegetable cart is no gold-mine," Joey often heard him say.

Now Joey wished he could have *his* picture in the paper. Maybe then Mr. Polaski would get a promotion, too.

He thought and he thought, but he couldn't decide how to go about it.

"How do you get to be a hero?" he said timidly to Brownie.

"Save a man's life, like me," answered Brownie.

"Did you rescue him from a burning building?" asked Joey, who had a romantic mind.

"Not at all," Brownie snorted. "I saved his life by not stepping on him. When a crowd pushed him, he fell under my feet. And I stood still as a statue. It's the way they taught me in school."

He looked so pleased with himself that Joey decided just standing still must be quite difficult for a Police Horse.

But the Percheron nearly strangled on his oats.

"Think of the lives *I've* saved," he whispered to Joey. "Thousands and thousands! Why, the city is *filled* with people I haven't stepped on."

But Joey didn't laugh. He just went on wondering how he could be a hero and get his picture in the paper.

Whenever he saw a crowd he trotted toward it, hoping somebody would fall under his feet. But Mr. Polaski always pulled him back to the curb again. And although he stood as quietly as a statue while Mr. Polaski sold his vegetables, *that* didn't make him a hero. It just brought him pats on the nose and an extra carrot or two.

Once a lady with a camera took his picture as he was nibbling a lump of sugar from the

hand of a friendly little girl. Unluckily, a fly was
buzzing around him and he had to swish his
tail and wrinkle his nose just as the lady snapped
the shutter. So probably it wasn't a good likeness. At any rate, he didn't hear of the picture's
appearing in any paper.

Then one day he thought his chance had come.

Mr. Polaski was selling a cauliflower to a woman in front of an apartment house and Joey was saying hello to a pigeon.

Suddenly a little boy, just learning to walk, came down the apartment house steps ahead of his nurse, and wobbled into the street. It was a busy street, with cars whizzing by and trucks rushing to reach the corner before the light turned red.

The nurse called to the little boy but he didn't stop. The lady was too busy pinching the cauliflower to notice him. And Mr. Polaski was too busy with the lady.

But Joey saw. And quick as a flash, he reached out and caught the little boy by the seat of his bright blue sun-suit.

"Now I'm a hero!" he thought to himself, "And my picture will surely be in the paper."

But the little boy began to cry and the nurse came running after him, shrieking, "Help!" The lady dropped the cauliflower and said, "I do believe your horse bit that child!"

And since Mr. Polaski hadn't been watching, he couldn't explain that Joey was only rescuing the little boy from the cars and the trucks.

Mr. Polaski had to apologize to the nurse, and on the way down the street he scolded Joey as if he had done something wrong.

"A vegetable cart isn't a gold-mine," he said crossly. "And now you have lost me a customer." And he didn't even give Joey an apple with his lunch.

Joey knew Mr. Polaski didn't understand, and forgave him. But it made him quite down-hearted.

"How am I to get my picture in the paper?" he asked the Percheron that night.

"Join a circus!" snapped the Percheron, throwing a bit of hay crossly onto the floor. He

was fond of Joey but he believed that Brownie was putting foolish ideas into his head.

"Join a circus," Joey said to himself, thoughtfully. "Why yes, circus horses *do* get their pictures in the paper. I could learn to walk on my hind legs and do tricks."

But when he practiced walking on his hind legs in the stall, he frightened the man

who was bringing him his oats.

And after he had tried to bow and kneel on one leg as he had heard that circus horses do, he ached so badly all over that he limped as he pulled the cart.

So he had to give up the idea of becoming a circus performer. But his hope of helping Mr. Polaski led him into trouble one June morning.

It was a very pleasant morning. Joey was jogging along, enjoying the sunshine, while Mr. Polaski from the front seat of the cart sang out, "Strawberries! Strawberries! Nice fresh Strawberries!"

A lady called to them from the upstairs window of a house and Mr. Polaski, stopping the cart, climbed the steps to sell her two boxes of berries. He left Joey standing still as a statue.

But just as Mr. Polaski was counting his change in the hall, Joey heard a sound that made his ears stand straight up on his head. It was the exciting sound of trumpets and drums and marching feet.

"A parade," thought Joey. He knew about parades. Brownie had often told him that the

horse who led one was bound to have his picture taken. It was like a law.

"Boom!" went the drums. "Tarara, tum-tum, tara!" tootled the horns and the bugles. It was too much for Joey.

Lifting his feet smartly and trailing his reins to one side, off he trotted in the direction of the music. He reached the corner just as the marchers reached it, too. The crowds watching the parade were too surprised to stop him. Even the policemen noticed him too late. Before they knew it, Joey was there at the head of the line, ready to lead the paraders up the avenue.

The only trouble was that he had taken a left turn while the parade was trying to turn to the right. There he was in the way of everybody!

The fife-players stopped so suddenly that the buglers stepped on their heels. The drummers stepped on the heels of the buglers. And the men who were only marching, stepped on the heels of the drummers. The whole

parade came to a standstill.

When Mr. Polaski ran panting up to the corner, the policeman was holding Joey by the bridle, the crowd was laughing, and the paraders were very angry. It was a dreadful moment.

Mr. Polaski explained that Joey meant no harm. So the policeman let them go with a warning and the parade started up again. But Mr. Polaski seemed so frightened and upset that Joey realized he had made a terrible mistake.

"Whatever has got into you, Joey?" asked Mr. Polaski, sorrowfully. "A vegetable-cart is no gold-mine. But you'll make me poorer than I am, if you don't behave yourself. Then what will happen to my six children?"

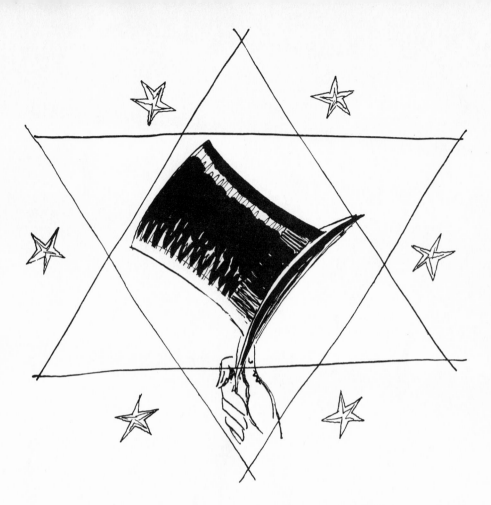

Poor Joey! He felt very sad; especially since Brownie's Sergeant had received another promotion and Brownie was prouder than ever. He swished his black tail and tossed his black mane and boasted about how well he had pushed back the crowds one day when the President of the United States drove by.

He even had his picture again—in the *Daily News*. He was leading a parade.

"I'll never be a hero and I'll never amount to anything," Joey confided to the Percheron. "I'm just an ordinary city horse with no talent. It's too bad for Mr. Polaski."

"You're a good fellow, Joey," said the Percheron. "Just cheer up and get that nonsense out of your head about newspaper pictures. Do your duty and everything will be all right."

So Joey made an effort to be cheerful and obedient, and Mr. Polaski didn't have to scold him again.

But things weren't going too well with the vegetable-cart. It was now the middle of the summer and very hot in the city. It was so hot that many of Mr. Polaski's best customers moved right out into the country to be comfortable. The vegetables and the fruit wilted in the heat, and new customers would not buy them. But Mr. Polaski's six children ate just as much as ever and needed as many pairs of shoes.

So. Mr. Polaski's face grew longer and longer.

One morning, earlier than usual, Mr. Polaski came into the stable and took Joey out to the cart.

"We're going to New Jersey, Joey," he said as he fastened the harness and put a hat over Joey's ears to keep off the sun. "I've heard of a place where I can get fresh vegetables cheaper than here. We'll drive over and look at them."

Joey was pleased to be having an adventure. In spite of the heat, he trotted along briskly in the direction that Mr. Polaski told him was New Jersey.

He trotted for blocks and blocks, weaving his way through the throngs of cars and trucks and busses. The streets were new and exciting to him and he liked it when they came to one which ran as far as he could see, beside a river.

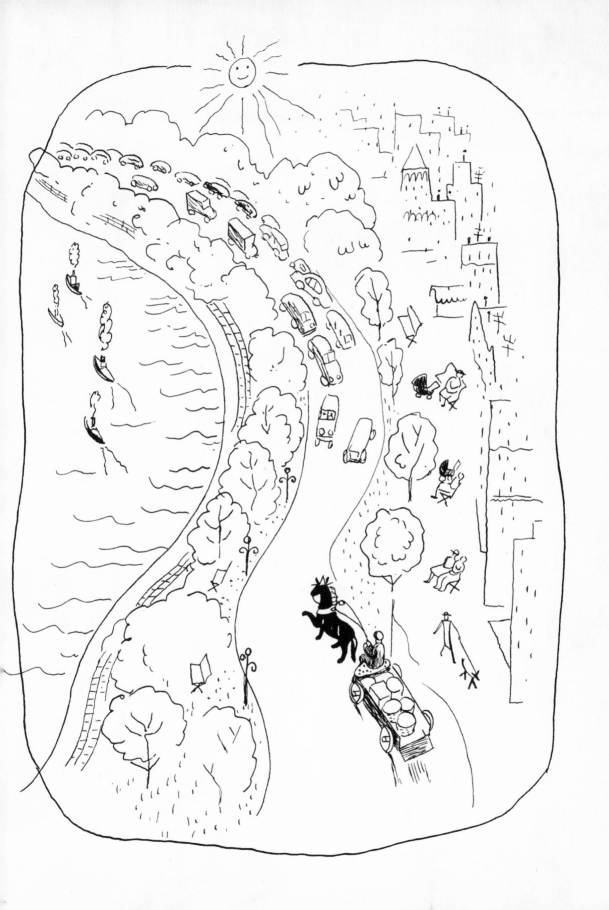

Finally he trotted up a sort of hill and all of a sudden found himself on a great bridge flung across the water. It might have frightened

another horse but Joey wasn't frightened at all.
He only slowed to a walk, the better to enjoy
the sight of the river and the boats skimming
busily along below him.

Mr. Polaski enjoyed it too, and they were both sorry to see the toll-house at the end of the bridge coming into sight. There seemed to be a crowd gathered there; and the cars, too, were moving slowly. Joey hurried a little so he could see what was going on. In fact, he edged right in front of a truck which was shifting gears, and the driver shouted at him. But Joey didn't mind, he was so interested.

The cart stopped at the toll-house, which was decorated with flags. And then, just as Mr. Polaski started to take out his purse to pay the toll, a man with a red carnation in his button-hole stepped up to them.

He wore a silk hat and carried a bouquet of flowers. Behind him came several other men, some with cameras and some with pencils and pads of paper in their hands.

"Congratulations!" said the man with the silk hat. "These flowers are for you. You have also won the fifty-dollar prize. What is your name, sir?"

"Polaski," said Mr. Polaski, much surprised. "Please—I don't understand."

"We are from the Department of Bridges," the man said, "and this prize is being given to the millionth vehicle to pass the toll-house.

999,995   999,996   999,997

Your cart was the millionth."

999,998   999,999   1,000,000 !!

"And we're reporters," said one of the men who carried pencils and paper. "We'd like your address, too. There's quite a story for our papers in this. You see we had expected a car or a truck or a bus to get the award. We didn't count on a horse and cart."

"What's your horse's name?" another reporter asked. When Mr. Polaski told him, he wrote down 'Joey' on the pad of paper. Then he shook Mr. Polaski's hand and several people cheered.

It was almost as good as leading a parade. The first man put the flowers in front of the cart and handed Mr. Polaski five ten-dollar bills. Then the men with cameras crowded around and cars halted to watch and people shouted cheerful remarks.

"Smile, now," said a cameraman. "And hold on to your horse. We especially want a good shot of him."

"That's quite a bonnet he's wearing," said another. "But he needs just one more touch. He's the hero of the day, you know."

He whispered something to the man in the silk hat. Then that gentleman took the red carnation out of his buttonhole and tucked it behind Joey's ear.

"Don't let him move," said the cameraman. But Joey wouldn't have moved for anything, not even for a hundred flies. He stood still as a statue and looked straight into the cameras, while the bulbs flashed like fireworks. He wasn't going to take a chance on spoiling *this* picture.

Afterwards the reporters patted his neck and complimented Mr. Polaski on driving such a well-behaved horse.

"We're holding up traffic, I'm afraid," said the silk-hatted man. "You'll have to move on. But look in the papers tomorrow—you'll be sure to see yourselves."

And with everybody gaily waving and the cars tooting their horns good-naturedly, Mr. Polaski and Joey moved on.

When they got back to the stable that night, Joey didn't say a word to the other horses about his adventure. Something might go wrong—perhaps the papers wouldn't use the picture after all. Besides, he was afraid his hat wasn't really becoming.

But the next morning Mr. Polaski burst in, waving half a dozen newspapers.

"Look, Joey!" he cried. "Here we are! We're famous!" He opened one of the papers and there, almost on the front page was a picture of Joey, handsome as a circus horse, with his hat becomingly tilted, and the red carnation behind his ear.

Underneath the picture it said:

NEW YORK ONLY ONE-HORSE TOWN
AFTER ALL—CART-HORSE JOEY WINS
FIFTY DOLLAR PRIZE

All the horses craned their necks over their stalls to see. Even Brownie was impressed. He murmured, "Excellent likeness." And the Percheron said dryly, "Well, you made it."

"But that's not all, Joey," Mr. Polaski said. "Maybe a vegetable-cart *is* a gold-mine after all. A friend of mine—he knew me in the old country—saw that picture first thing this morning and he telephoned me right away. He's got a farm on Long Island and he needs somebody to help him in the city. He says I'll be his partner. Every day he'll bring me his fresh vegetables and you and I will sell them. Now I won't mind if my six children grow so fast out of their shoes."

My, but Joey was happy! He said later to the Percheron, "Of course it would have been nice to have been a real hero. But I expect this is nearly as good."

"There are all sorts of ways of being a hero," the Percheron told him kindly. "You did your duty every day and didn't complain and that's as good a way as *I* know of. And," he added with a side glance at Brownie, still tossing his black mane in the right-hand stall, "it's certainly just as good as saving a man's life by standing still."

"Anyhow," said Joey contentedly, "I got Mr. Polaski his promotion."